G. Russell Reynolds

Rusty and the Circus of Doubt

Rusty and
the Circus of Doubt

by G. Russell Reynolds

Illustrations by Sherrie Molitor

To Melea and Grant. Never let other's opinions, shortcomings, limitations or circumstances define you or become your own. There is greatness inside of you. There always has been. You just have to believe…

I love you,
Uncle Russell

Rusty was a small boy. Well, he was actually an elephant. A small boy elephant who lived in the circus. But Rusty never felt like he belonged in the circus. He felt that he was meant for more than this, for something different.

The other elephants laughed at him for such ideas. "What, do you think you're special?" one elephant asked.

"Well…yeah. Don't you?" replied Rusty.

But they just laughed and teased him more.

During the day, the Circus Boss would train them to do what circus elephants were supposed to do. At least what *he* thought they were supposed to do. The boss was sometimes mean when Rusty didn't fit in and follow the others. He would threaten Rusty by cracking his whip in the air and yell, "Not too slow! Not too fast! Extend your trunk! Extend your tail! Be long, Rusty! You must be-long!"

At night, Rusty was held by a big old chain attached to a big old metal spike pounded deep in the ground. Wanting to be free, he would pull and pull on the chain, but it was no use. The chain was too big, and he was too small.

"Who do you think you are?!" bellowed Lion from his corner.

"Huh?" said Rusty timidly.

"Do you think you're better than us? Better than *me*?"

"N-n-no…" said Rusty, "I just…"

"I am the King of the jungle!" said Lion, "and if I'm not getting out of here, neither are you!"

"B-b-but…" Rusty said nervously. "We're not in the jungle."

"Whhhhaaat?!" roared Lion.

"Well, I mean, wouldn't you be happier if we were? Because maybe then you would really be a king instead of…"

"RRRROAR!"

Rusty gulped hard as he realized he had said too much.

"Listen here you little runt…" said Lion as he came closer with his teeth gleaming in the moonlight.

Suddenly, the door flew open and the Circus Boss stood there in his pajamas, angry at being woken up by all the noise. "Rusty! What have you done now?!"

The next day, Rusty was only given half the food that the other elephants got. As he sat quietly eating, Zebra came over and sat next to him. "Not fair, not fair at all. This whole circus is a joke! And to treat you like that? Pbpbhhh."

Rusty became excited that somebody understood how he felt!

But then Lion walked by, glaring at them. "What's going on here?"

"N-n-nothing." Said Zebra with a big smile, hoping not to upset Lion. He looked down at Rusty and said, "Stupid elephant! Trying to talk to me." And with that he walked away quickly making sure not to go too near to Lion.

Lion simply turned his nose up at Rusty with a "Humpff."

And walked away.

As the days became weeks and the weeks became months, Rusty became sad. He stopped trying to pull on his chain. He stopped talking to the others about his dreams beyond the circus. What was the point? Maybe it really was better just to fit in and belong. It was certainly better than feeling so lonely and wanting a dream that he couldn't have. But the dream didn't go away. It filled his head at night as he tried to go to sleep.

One night as he tossed and turned, he said aloud to no one in particular, "Oh, I don't know what to do! I wish somebody could help me."

"I can help you." came a voice from the dark.

"Who's there?" asked Rusty.

"*You* are there. *I* am here." Said the monkey, stepping into the light.

"What?" asked Rusty.

"You asked who is there. You are there, and I am here." Replied Monkey.

"No, I am here." Rusty responded.

"Yes, you are." Said Monkey.

"I'm confused." Said Rusty.

"Right again." Said Monkey.

Rusty tried to outsmart the clever monkey, "Okay, I am here, and you *WERE* there, but now that you're here, we're in the same place."

"*Are we?...*" asked Monkey.

Rusty gave up, "Aww, what do you want anyway?"

Monkey responded, "The question is, what do *you* want? You wished for someone to help you, so here I am. What do you want?"

"You're the answer to my wish?" Rusty asked skeptically.

"No, actually you are." replied Monkey, "But let's stay on point. What do you want?"

Rusty hung his head, "It doesn't matter, I can't have what I want. Everybody says so."

"And you believed them? Pity…"

"Look, I'm stuck here!" said Rusty tugging on his chain.

"I have the key." Said Monkey with a gleam in his eye.

"The key to my chain?" Rusty asked with wonderment.

"The key to your freedom!" exclaimed Monkey.

But Rusty didn't trust the monkey yet. "I don't see any key…"

Monkey replied, "Why, it's in my very name! I am the mon-key! I am the mon-key, with the one key, to set you freeeeee!" Monkey rolled on the ground laughing and being quite amused with his little rhyme.

Rusty started giggling too. The monkey was pretty funny, and Rusty could use a good laugh after everything he'd been through.

"There, see?" said Monkey. "Better already. It's good medicine, laughter. Quite healing. I recommend a daily dose." Monkey pretended to take a spoon of laughter and fell on the ground in another fit of giggles.

"Okay, okay…" said Rusty, "but how do we set me free?"

"For now," said Monkey, "rest and just believe that it's possible."

"It is?" asked Rusty.

"Anything is possible, if you believe." replied Monkey. "Rest now. More to come soon. More to come…" and with that, monkey faded into the shadows.

The next day was business as usual with work under the watchful eye of the Circus Boss. Rusty wondered if he even saw the monkey at all or if it was just a dream. But then, as the Circus Boss shouted, "Belong, Rusty!"

Monkey popped out from behind a barrel and whispered, "No, *believe*, Rusty!" Rusty was so surprised by Monkey's appearance that he forgot what he was doing and brought the whole formation to a crashing halt.

"Rrrruuuusty!!!" shouted the Circus Boss, "Look what you've done! Go back to your tent! NO LUNCH!"

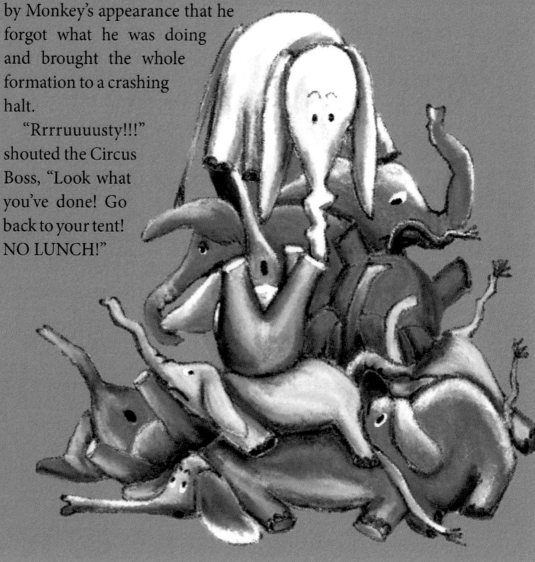

"Aww, man! A lot of good that did me." Rusty said to Monkey, as they walked back towards the tent.

"Actually, it did." said Monkey. "How so?" asked Rusty. "Now you have the day off!" Monkey replied with a smile. "Sometimes blessings, they come in disguise. But if you're looking for them, you can find them. Yes, that's the key, to always be looking for them."

Rusty responded, "Yeah, but I messed up the whole formation and got in trouble because I tried to believe instead of belong with all the others."

"Ah, so what?" said Monkey. "Funny thing about believing, it often disrupts the system that was built on the very fact that you didn't."

Rusty shook his head. He didn't always understand Monkey, but on some level, knew that what he said made sense.

Monkey just smiled. "Come with me." He said as he led Rusty away from the big tent and through the circus grounds.

Rusty saw many things he had never seen before, many interesting people and things. Finally, they came to stop in front of the Funhouse. A wise looking old gypsy woman sat in front.

"What brings you here?" she asked, looking at them suspiciously.

"He is here for the mirror!" replied Monkey with a wink of his eye.

"Do you think he is ready?" the gypsy woman replied.

Monkey eyed Rusty up and down and said, "We'll see..."

"Wait…" Rusty said, "ready for what?"

Monkey and the gypsy woman answered dramatically in unison, "THE MIRROR OF TRUTH!" Monkey continued, "Go inside and look into the mirror. Then come back and tell us what you see."

"Uhh….oh-okay." Said Rusty.

He was feeling a little nervous as he walked through the Funhouse. In fact, it didn't feel very fun at all. All of the strange colors, shapes, and shadows made him feel small. And as he approached the strange mirror, that's exactly what he saw; a small, scared, weak little elephant. No matter which way he turned or what angle he looked from, what he saw was not good enough.

Rusty's shoulders drooped even further as he hung his head and walked out.

"Well?..." asked Monkey. Then, "Oh…" as he saw Rusty's face.

The gypsy woman said, "He was not ready."

"Soon. Soon he will be." Replied Monkey with a gentle smile as he put his arm around Rusty, and they began to walk back to the tent.

Rusty's trunk dragged along the ground in disappointment as he walked.

"So?" Monkey asked, "What did you see?"

Rusty answered, "A small, scared, weak little runt… me. I saw the truth."

"*The* truth?" asked Monkey, "No, no, no… you saw *your* truth."

"I don't understand." said Rusty.

Monkey explained, "The mirror of truth doesn't show you *the* truth, it only shows you *your* truth. *THE* truth is way too big to be contained in a silly little mirror." Monkey saw that Rusty still looked confused. "Dear boy, the mirror of truth only shows you the truth that you show to it."

"B-but…" Rusty tried to interrupt as Monkey continued, "You went in feeling small, scared, unsure and defeated, so that's exactly what you saw."

Rusty said, "So you're saying if I had stepped up to the mirror, feeling majestic, proud and powerful that I would have seen…"

"Exactly that!" exclaimed Monkey. "That's how the mirror and life are the same. It only offers a reflection of what you are offering it."

Rusty said, "So, you think changing my thoughts would change my reflection? Or the world around me? Ha! That's crazy!"

"Is it?" Monkey asked, "Maybe what's crazy is thinking it wouldn't. Walking around in life thinking that what's going on outside has nothing to do with what's going on inside." he said tapping Rusty on the forehead.

"Hmmmm…" Rusty thought about what Monkey had said. "But the others said I wasn't special and that I should just belong."

"And you believed them?" asked Monkey in surprise.

"Lion said it too, and he said I was a little runt."

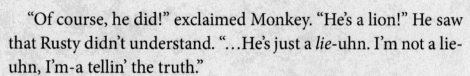

"Of course, he did!" exclaimed Monkey. "He's a lion!" He saw that Rusty didn't understand. "…He's just a *lie*-uhn. I'm not a lie-uhn, I'm-a tellin' the truth."

"Ooooohhh…" said Rusty as he realized what Monkey meant. "But what about Zebra? He said I was a stupid elephant, even though he seemed like he was on my side at first …until Lion walked by."

"Ha!" Monkey laughed, then asked, "What color is Zebra? Is he black or is he white?"

"Uhh…both?" said Rusty.

"Both but neither." Said Monkey. "Zebra will be either black or white, whichever will help him avoid a fight."

Rusty pondered what Monkey said as Monkey continued, "Zebra is a herd animal, not one for conflict. So, he'll always go with the group, or whoever's closest, or scariest, or most popular. To invest in his opinion is like investing in the wind blowing in only one direction."

As they approached Rusty's tent, Monkey said, with a gleam in his eye, "Listen, everybody who told you that you weren't special, or told you that you were small, or stupid, or not good enough or anything less than amazing, had a reason for doing so. And it had nothing to do with you."

Rusty was stopped in his tracks with this one. "How can it have nothing to do with me? It was all about me!"

"That's what I want you to figure out," Monkey replied.

Over the next days, Rusty watched and listened to all of the others, looking for a clue to Monkey's riddle. Through his observation, his awareness grew, and he began to see and hear things he had never noticed before. He grew very excited to tell Monkey what he had discovered.

Days later, when Monkey finally came to his tent, Rusty could hardly contain himself. "Monkey! Monkey! I understand! I saw how it has nothing to do with me!"

Monkey laughed as Rusty bounced up and down, "Okay, my boy. I can't wait to hear. Tell me!"

"Well," said Rusty, "The Circus Boss makes everybody feel small and less than him because if he didn't, nobody would put up with being treated that way and they would all leave his circus."

"Very good!" Monkey exclaimed. "Sadly, many bosses work that way, they control others through fear..."

Rusty cut him off in his excitement, "And Lion, woah! Lion is the same way! Lion gets his power by taking everybody else's! By pushing everyone else down, he makes himself feel big. That's why he says he's the king."

Monkey asked, "Do you think that's the way a real king would act?"

Rusty thought and then said, "No. He's not really a king, is he?"

"And on some level, I'll bet he knows that. And I'd bet that hurts." replied Monkey.

"That's probably what makes him so angry." Rusty said. And then, "Wow, I wonder what he would see if he looked in the Mirror of Truth…"

Monkey smiled at Rusty's growing awareness.

Then Rusty burst out again, "Oh! And Zebra! You were right about Zebra! He'll agree with anything, even if he just agreed with the opposite thing five minutes before!"

"What do you think he's really afraid of?" asked Monkey.

Rusty thought about it, then said, "Probably of not being liked, because he tries so hard to be liked by everyone."

"Or maybe of being alone." Said Monkey, "Maybe afraid of what he would see if he was."

Rusty sat down and said, "Wow. It sure does make it easier not to take it personally anymore when you know all this, huh?"

"Mmm-hmm." said Monkey.

Rusty said, "I saw that all of the others said I wasn't special because the truth is, *they're* not special!"

"Oh, but they are, my dear boy!" Monkey interjected.

"They are?" Rusty asked.

"Of course!" said Monkey, "Everyone has the potential to be special, just like you. They've just chosen to live their lives like they're not."

This made Rusty wonder, "But why? Why would they do that?" he asked.

"They don't even know they are doing it most of the time. Well, on some level they do, but it's because they don't believe. They don't *believe* they're special. They believe…"

Rusty finished Monkey's sentence, "That they're not good enough."

"Yes." Said Monkey, "Maybe someone told them that they weren't, and they believed them. They believed the lie instead of the truth of who they *really* are….Sound familiar?"

It sounded all too familiar to Rusty.

Monkey smiled and said, "Sleep now, Rusty. There is more to come soon. Keep looking deeply. There is more for you to see…"

Rusty continued to watch the others as they all played their parts in the Circus of Doubt. But now, instead of looking at them with hurt or resentment, he looked at them with compassion. Even when they were mean to him, Rusty just smiled and walked away because he knew how sad or in pain they were on the inside.

When he saw Monkey again, Monkey asked him, "Well, what else have you seen?"

"Most others in the Circus aren't very happy. That's why they were mean to me, or to anybody. So, it really does have nothing to do with me. I don't feel sad or hurt anymore, even if they say things that hurt me or made me sad before. I know who I am now."

Monkey smiled, "Ahh, you have discovered something very important. No one can take your power, no one can take your joy…"

Rusty jumped in, "Unless I give it to them!"

Monkey laughed, "Exactly right, dear boy. And the only way the words or opinions of others can have any effect over you?"

"Is if I agree with them!" Rusty answered.

Monkey smiled proudly and said, "Come on. I think it's time to visit an old friend."

As they approached the Fun House, Rusty felt much different than he did the first time.

The old gypsy woman nodded as they approached. "Do you think he's ready?" she asked.

"Doesn't really matter what I think." Monkey answered with a wink.

"I'm ready." Rusty said with confidence.

The old gypsy woman nodded again with approval and pulled back the curtain for Rusty to enter. As Rusty walked down the strange corridor, he saw the strange colors, shapes and shadows that had intimidated him before. They were still a little frightening, but Rusty pushed through the fear and kept moving forward anyway. "Besides," he thought, "Shadows are nothing to be afraid of, they're just an absence of light."

And Rusty had a new light inside of him that shone through shadows and fears alike.

As he stepped up to the mirror, at first, he saw the same small elephant he had seen before. But then he said, "No. Only if I agree with it." Rusty took a deep breath and stood tall and proud. The mirror changed before his eyes! Standing before him was the most majestic, powerful elephant Rusty had ever seen! Rusty took another deep breath as he soaked it in. "This is real. This is the truth. *This is my truth now.*"

As Rusty stepped out of the Fun House, Monkey didn't even have to ask what he had seen. He could see it in Rusty's eyes and in the way he carried himself.

"Woo hoo!" squealed Monkey, as he did a flip and started dancing a jig.

Rusty laughed, as Monkey and the old gypsy woman began clapping for him.

"More than ready!" said the gypsy as they all laughed and Rusty beamed with pride.

Walking back to the tent, Rusty asked Monkey, "What about all the others?" "What about them?" asked Monkey.

"Well, I don't think I can hide this." said Rusty.

"Why in the world would you want to?" exclaimed Monkey.

"It's just," said Rusty, "I don't know how well they'll react to it."

Monkey looked at him and said, "You can't expect them all to. After all, you shining your truth is directly challenging their Circus of Doubt. But that's not for you to worry about or fix. You just shine bright, be the example. Be your amazing self. Maybe they get it, maybe they don't."

They both smiled and kept walking.

Suddenly, Lion jumped out from behind one of the other tents. "And where exactly have *you* been?!" he said with a growl. "Running around with that stupid old monkey, filling your head with garbage and lies?!"

Rusty stuttered in response, "W-what? N-n-no, he's not…"

"SILENCE!" roared Lion.

Monkey just crossed his arms and rolled his eyes as he leaned up against a nearby barrel with a sigh.

"I'm not sure which I want to do more," Lion said as he moved slowly and threateningly towards Rusty, "turn you in to the Circus Boss, or rip you to pieces myself!"

Rusty started to tremble and back away. He was still afraid of Lion, and the present circumstances made it hard to remember what he had experienced in the Fun House.

As Lion got closer, Monkey casually leaned over and whispered in Rusty's ear, "You know, in the wild, there's only one time a lion would dare attack an elephant alone; when he's small. You are *not* small. Remember who you are, who you *really* are, and *believe…*"

Rusty stopped backing up when he remembered what he had discovered about Lion in the days before. He stopped backing up and stood tall when he remembered the powerful, majestic elephant he had seen in the mirror.

When Lion saw this he roared, "You dare stand against me?!"

Rusty took a deep breath and said calmly, "No. *You* dare to stand against *me*."

With a mighty roar, Lion leapt in the air to pounce on Rusty and rip him to pieces! But Rusty took another deep breath and let out a trumpet blast from his trunk that dwarfed Lion's roar and was so powerful that it sent Lion flying backwards in the other direction and into the side of another tent that came crashing down around him!

Hearing the commotion, some of the others came outside to see what was happening. Lion got up and stumbled out of the wreckage, dizzy and disoriented. When he saw that the others were watching, he felt embarrassed and angry and got ready to pounce again.

"Why you little…" but before Lion could finish his sentence, Rusty lifted his foot high up in the air and stomped it on the ground so hard that it shook Lion, it shook the others, it shook the tents, and it shook the ground itself!

"I am NOT little!" said Rusty in a powerful commanding voice. "And *you*… are a bad kitty. Now go away."

Lion gulped hard at the sight of Rusty, now a fully-grown elephant, towering over him. He looked around at all of the others who were watching. Some of them were in shock, some in approval, and some were holding back laughter. Lion felt very small all of a sudden as he looked back up at Rusty, now a fully-grown elephant, and realized that the smartest thing he could do, was exactly what Rusty had told him to do.

And that's exactly what he did; run away. The others cheered and applauded Rusty saying things like, "Rusty the great!" "Rusty the invincible!" and "Rusty the lion tamer!"

That night in his tent, Rusty felt proud of himself for standing up to Lion and grateful for all that he had learned. He playfully tossed his chain back and forth as Monkey came in.

"What a day, what a day." said Monkey with his usual grin.

"Yes indeed." answered Rusty.

"You have seen things. You have seen the truth." said Monkey.

"Yes." said Rusty.

"You are powerful now. And why is that?" asked Monkey.

"Because I believe I am." answered Rusty.

"Yes, yes," said Monkey, "What you believe sets the stage for your whole life. If you believe you are small, you are small. If you believe you are powerful, you are powerful. If you believe you are free…"

At the thought of freedom, Rusty looked down and started playing with his chain again.

Monkey smiled knowingly and asked, "What is it, Rusty?"

Rusty thought for a moment and said, "Monkey, I saw the others tonight and for the first time I noticed something I hadn't seen before. I saw that the other adult elephants aren't bound with a chain. They're only tied in place by a tiny rope."

Monkey replied, "Ahh, your vision has become clearer."

Rusty continued, "But why would the smallest and youngest elephants be bound with a big chain and the biggest and most powerful elephants be tied with a tiny rope? It doesn't make any sense. They could break free easily. Why don't they?"

Monkey looked Rusty deep in the eye and said, "Because they don't believe that they can. From their youth, they are taught to believe that the chain is stronger than them and that they can never break free. Once they come to believe that as the truth, a chain is no longer necessary, only a tiny rope."

Rusty thought about this for a moment, then said, "But…then why am I still held by this big old chain?"

Monkey looked at Rusty with love and a gleam in his eye and asked, "Are you?…"

With wonder, Rusty looked down again and saw that he was really only tied with a tiny rope! "W-w-w-what?!" exclaimed Rusty. "But…but…that was a big old chain! What happened?! Is this magic?"

Monkey smiled and said, "No magic. It was only a big old chain because you still believed it was. Now you see the truth, because now you believe in something different. Now, you believe in you more than the Circus of Doubt. You believe in *you*. The key to your freedom."

With a tear in his eye, Rusty lifted his foot and pulled the rope taut. He looked back at Monkey, "I'm scared."

Monkey smiled and said, "Check again. Maybe that's just excitement in disguise."

Rusty nodded and lifted his foot even higher, pulling the rope even tighter until 'POP!' it snapped in two. "It wasn't even that hard to do." Rusty thought after he had done it. He easily shook the remaining piece of rope off of his foot and watched as it fell to the ground. "I'm free." he said to Monkey with wonder and joy.

"You always have been, my friend." replied Monkey. "Now, where will you go? What will you do? Who will you become? Anything is possible. You just have to believe…"

"And *you*. Yes you, reading this book. Surely you don't believe in that old chain and your Circus of Doubt anymore? Not more than yourself, do you? Ha ha, I didn't think so. So now, where will you go? What will you do? And who will you become? Anything is possible. You just have to believe…"

The End

...for now.

Acknowledgments

I would like to acknowledge my mother, Diana Simone, originator of the Amber Alert for Missing Children for her gift to children, parents and humanity and for being a shining example that one person can make a difference.

My aunt Judy Keel for her continuous encouragement and assistance in bringing this book to be when I might have let the idea go.

All of the loved ones past and present who have believed in me and believed this book was a message worth sharing.

To all of the animals in my Circus of Doubt who gave me enough contrast and pain to know that there must be more, and to seek out the greatness within me.

Made in the USA
Middletown, DE
11 July 2019